BENARES

Ganges

Ganges

The Ganges fell from Heaven,
and her fall was softened
by the long locks of the god Shiva. . . .

Sacred River

Sacred River

Written and Illustrated by TED LEWIN

CLARION BOOKS/*New York*

Clarion Books
a Houghton Mifflin Company imprint
215 Park Avenue South, New York, NY 10003
Text and illustrations copyright © 1995 by Ted Lewin

The illustrations for this book were executed in watercolor on Strathmore Bristol.
The text was set in 17/20-point Centaur.

Printed in the USA

Library of Congress Cataloging-in-Publication Data
Lewin, Ted.
Sacred river / written and illustrated by Ted Lewin.
p.   cm.
ISBN 0-395-69846-4
1. Ganges River (India and Bangladesh)—Description and travel—Juvenile
literature.   2. Ganges River Valley (India and Bangladesh)—Description
and travel—Juvenile literature.   I. Title.
DS485.G25L49   1994
954'.1—dc20   94-18370
CIP
AC

HOR 10 9 8 7 6 5 4 3 2 1

There is a city in India called Benares. It is also known by two other names, Varanasi and Kashi, which means "resplendent with divine light." One of the oldest cities in the world, it was already ancient when Buddha visited there, around 500 B.C. Through it flows the mighty river Ganges. The Ganges descends from the Himalayas, the highest mountains in the world, on a long journey to the Bay of Bengal.

For Hindus, all rivers are places of worship and are sacred. The Ganges is the most sacred of all, and is celebrated by one hundred eight sacred names. Its waters are said to have the power of salvation.

The highest goal in the life of a Hindu is a pilgrimage to Benares. It is a way of achieving serenity and freedom from worldly problems and pain. Each year pilgrims come to Benares by the millions to purify their souls in the Ganges' sacred waters, as they have for many centuries.

Across the mile-wide sacred river, the life-giving sun rises on a new day. The old boatman rows away from the dark stone steps called ghats.

A forest of masts rises from the boats anchored near the ghats.

Hooded pilgrims hunch in long boats that slide by on the dark river.

The morning light slowly rises on the old walls of the maharajas'
palaces. It passes the dark stain of a high-water mark from past
monsoon floods.

Thousands of pilgrims pour down the ghats from the narrow streets above and spill out of the boats below.

As the sun rises, they wade into the water to be cleansed and purified by the sacred river.

They make offerings of jai flowers.

Holy men with painted faces sit cross-legged, praying beneath huge umbrellas.

The colorful clothing of the people makes a flower garden of the stone steps.

The umbrellas sit on the ghats like a huge mushroom patch. Above them rise minarets, towers, domes, and beyond, the old palaces of the maharajas of Amber and Jaipur.

The old boatman rows to the ghats, oars creaking in their locks. Boats jam in alongside, filled to the gunwales with pilgrims and festooned with jai flowers.

Women with red-painted feet step from the river and rewrap themselves
in dazzling saris, while overhead, flocks of black birds soar like spirit kites.

Just before a half-submerged temple tower, gray smoke and piles of ash mark the burning ghats, the place of funeral pyres. When Hindus die, their bodies are cremated and their ashes scattered upon the river.

Great, dark boats full of firewood wait to unload.

The souls of the faithful will continue onward, while their ashes join the jai flowers in the river on the long journey to the sea.